Brownies
D0656081

For Amber, who loves being
a 4th Haywards Heath Brownie

STRIPES PUBLISHING
An imprint of Magi Publications
1 The Coda Centre, 189 Munster Road,
London SW6 6AW

A paperback original. First published in Great Britain in 2010
Published by arrangement with Girlguiding UK

ISBN: 978-1-84715-119-3

A CIP catalogue record for this book is available
from the British Library.

Printed and bound in the UK.
2 4 6 8 10 9 7 5 3

Brownies

Dance Dash

Stripes

Meet the Brownies

Katie

Katie, Grace's twin, is super sporty and likes to play games and win. She wants to get every Brownie badge and her Six is Foxes!

Jamila

Jamila's got too many brothers, so she loves Brownies because NO BOYS ARE ALLOWED! Jamila is a Badger!

Ellie

Awesome at art and crafts, Ellie used to be a Rainbow and likes making new friends. Ellie is a Hedgehog!

Charlie

Animal-crazy Charlie has a guinea pig called Nibbles. She loves Brownie quizzes and Pow Wows. Her Six is Squirrels!

Grace

Grace is Katie's twin sister and she's ballet bonkers. Grace enjoys going on Brownie outings, and she is a Rabbit!

Brownies

Chapter 1

"Hey, look!" exclaimed Grace.

She was standing by the Brownie noticeboard in the school hall with Jamila, Katie, Ellie and Charlie – her best friends. It was Tuesday night – Brownie night!

"It's the photos of the big Girlguiding Badenbridge party," Grace continued. "The one that Brownies, Guides and Rainbows from all over the District went to."

"Oh, that was such a good party," Ellie sighed. "Look – that's us there!"

All the 1st Badenbridge Brownies had gone to the event, which was to mark the start of the Girlguiding UK Centenary celebrations.

Hundreds of girls had packed into the hall at Badenbridge Manor that afternoon!

"Imagine – there have been Brownies for nearly one hundred years," said Jamila. "That's such a long time."

"I'm sure that girls will *always* want to be Brownies, Guides and Rainbows," Katie said. "It's such fun!"

The others nodded in agreement.

"Oh, there's a photo here of Jasmine too!" said Ellie. "She's standing next to her winning sunflower with the mayor."

The annual sunflower competition involved all the Rainbow, Brownie and Guide units in Badenbridge, as well as Beavers, Cubs and Scouts. The idea was to grow a sunflower in a pot and then plant it in the school garden when it was big enough. The person who grew the tallest sunflower won a book token!

"Wasn't it brilliant that she won the competition?" said Katie. "She beat the boys!"

The year before, Ashvini's older brother had won. Ashvini said he hadn't stopped going on about how boys were best ever since.

"A victory for the girls," declared Jamila.

"And for the Brownies!" added Grace, grinning.

"Jessica!" Chloe cried suddenly.

The five Brownie friends looked across the hall and saw the other girls gathering excitedly around two visitors. One of them was Jessica, who used to be the Sixer of the Foxes, Katie's Six. She'd left Brownies a few months ago to move to Guides.

"Jessica's here!" Charlie exclaimed. "But who's with her?"

"That's Pip from school," said Ellie. "Isn't she Jessica's cousin?"

"Of course," said Jamila. "Now I remember – Jessica said she'd come back to see us when Pip joined Brownies. Let's go and say hello."

The five girls raced over.

"Hello, Jessica!" said Grace. "Wow, your Guides outfit is so cool!"

Jessica grinned. "Thanks," she said.

"Hi, Pip!" said Katie. "We're really pleased you're starting Brownies tonight – welcome!"

"Thanks," said Pip, smiling shyly.

"So, Jessica – what's Guides like?" asked Katie.

"It's really good fun," she replied. "We do games and songs, like at Brownies. I've been abseiling and I'm working for my Science badge too. Oh, and the most exciting thing is that we started on a new project last week.

It's called Adventure 100 and it's for the Girlguiding UK Centenary."

"Sounds great," said Grace.

"It is!" said Jessica. "I still miss Brownies but I really love Guides. I just wish I could come to both! Anyway, I've got to take Pip over to see Vicky and Sam, so I'd better go now or you won't be able to start the meeting. See you soon!"

"Bye!" The girls all waved.

"Guides sounds so cool," sighed Katie.

"Yeah," said Charlie. "I suppose the only good thing about one day being too old to be a Brownie is we'll have Guides to go to instead."

Jamila smiled. "Come on," she said. "We'd better get to our Six tables – quick!"

The Brownie meeting started with the Name Game. The Brownies often played this when new girls joined, to help them learn everyone's name. They stood in a circle with one girl in the middle holding a ball. She called out a Brownie's name and threw the ball to her before catching it back. Eventually, all the Brownies' names had been called out. It was really good fun and Pip laughed along with the others.

"Now, girls," said Vicky, one of the Brownie Leaders, taking the ball at the end of the game. "Time to sit in our Ring for a Pow Wow."

All the girls quickly sat down.

"First of all, I'd like to officially welcome Pip, who has joined us at Brownies tonight," said Sam, the other Leader.

Immediately, all the Brownies gave three

claps, saying "Welcome" each time they did. Pip smiled at them all.

"Daisy," Sam continued. "Would you like to give Pip her *Becoming a Brownie* book?"

Daisy, like Jessica, was a Guide, but she came along to help out at Brownies as a Young Leader.

She handed over the book to Pip, and as Daisy settled down again, Vicky said, "Now Pip, every girl who joins Brownies is given a Brownie Buddy who answers her questions and helps her to get to know all the things that happen at our meetings. We're going to put you in Foxes."

Katie and all the other Foxes sat up straight, proud that Pip was joining them.

"And your Brownie Buddy is going to be … Katie!"

Katie looked at Pip and grinned from ear to ear, pleased that she had been asked to do such an important job.

"We've got lots more to talk about this evening," Vicky continued. "We'd like to tell you about an exciting new project we thought you might like to get involved in. It's called Adventure 100."

"Oh, Jessica was talking about that earlier," Boo pointed out. "She's doing it at Guides."

"That's right," said Sam. "All the Brownies, Guides and Rainbows can take part in it if they want to."

"What is Adventure 100?" asked Bethany.

"It's part of the Centenary celebrations," explained Vicky. "A chance to think about Girlguiding UK in the past, the present and the future."

"Cool!" said Caitlin, and the others agreed with her.

"We've been sent this brilliant poster," explained Sam, holding it up for all the Brownies to see. "It's a map that shows you all the adventures that we can have over the next twelve months."

The girls leaned forward to look at it closely.

It was a picture of an island featuring drawings of loads of little Brownies and other girls having fun – running races, putting on plays and exploring. Some illustrations – a Brownie at the top of a tower, two sets of eyes peering through the dark, a red and white life ring, a theatrical mask, a rocket, a penguin on an ice cube, a wheel, a clown with the number 100, a pair of clasped hands and a trefoil badge – popped up several times on the map, and each little drawing had a title next to it.

"There are ten sections in Adventure 100, and each section is made up of ten tasks," Sam continued. "The idea is that you choose at least one task from each section to win points – some tasks are worth five points, others are worth ten."

"Win points?" asked Katie. "Does that mean it's a competition?"

"No, it isn't a competition," said Vicky, "and you don't have to finish bits in a set time either. But if you do manage to gain one hundred points, then you will be awarded the special Adventure 100 badge at the end of the Centenary year."

"Each one of you can choose whether you want to take part," Sam added. "If you don't want to, you don't have to. You can do some of the challenges on your own, or with

your Six, or we can work on things together as a unit. Oh, and Vicky and I, and all the other Leaders, are working towards Adventure 100 as well – except we have to earn one hundred and fifty points to get our badges!"

"So," said Vicky, "would any of you like to get involved?"

"Me!" said every Brownie in the room, waving their arms.

"Great!" said Sam, laughing. "And we've also got some good news – we've managed to get our first points towards Adventure 100 already, without even realizing it!"

The Brownies looked at her, puzzled.

"One section is called 'Share the Adventure'," explained Sam. "And by going to the District Centenary party with all those other units back in September, we all gained ten points each!"

"Yesss!" the Brownies cheered.

"And those of you who come on our unit camp later in the year can gain another ten points because it will count towards the section called 'Your Own Adventure'," added Vicky.

"This is great!" said Katie, who especially loved working on badges.

"We've got these lovely booklets for you," Sam revealed. "Daisy is going to hand them out. They contain details of special Centenary events that are coming up, plus lots of fun facts on guiding. You can also read about Adventure 100 and use the booklets as scrapbooks. Why don't you take a look at them before next week? Then we can talk a bit more about other tasks that you'd like to work on over the coming year."

Daisy handed each Brownie a copy of the colourful booklet, called *The Greatest Adventure*.

"There's a fantastic website too," she said. "We looked at it during Guides the other night."

"Oh yes," said Vicky. "Thanks for reminding me! Why not take a look at it? You'll be able to find the address in your booklets."

"Right," said Sam. "As you all think you'd like to get involved, why don't we make a start tonight!"

There was a buzz of excitement around the hall.

"One section of Adventure 100 is called 'In the Dark'," Sam explained.

"Is it scary?" wondered Lauren.

"Not at all!" said Vicky. "It's all about having fun at night time – like sleepovers, midnight feasts and night hikes."

"One of the tasks is to make some dreamcatchers," explained Sam. "When we have finished them, we can hang them in our bedroom windows at home to reflect our dreams about Brownies in the past, and Brownies around the world now and in the future."

"And to make sure we all have good dreams, of course! Shall we get started?" asked Vicky.

"Yes!" said all the Brownies, rushing over to the Six tables, ready to begin their next adventure.

Chapter 2

Next day at breaktime, the girls gathered in the playground to chat about everything that'd happened at Brownies the night before.

"I can't wait to finish my dreamcatcher next week," said Ellie.

"Me neither! Or to find out more about Adventure 100," said Katie.

Jamila nodded. "It sounds really good. By the look of that map that Vicky and Sam had, there are masses of tasks to choose from."

"Ooh," said Charlie, "we should have a look at that website they mentioned."

"Why don't we do it after school today, when you all come round to our house for tea?" suggested Grace.

"Yes!" the others agreed.

"Hey, there's Pip," said Katie, looking across the playground. "I'm going to ask if she'd like to come and play with us."

"Good idea." Jamila grinned. "Come on – let's get the skipping rope out!"

"I really love that new book that Mr Cole read to us this afternoon," said Ellie.

Mr Cole was their class teacher. Everyone liked him because he made them laugh and his lessons were lots of fun. Each afternoon he read them a story.

"I can't wait to find out what's going to happen next," said Charlie, munching on some carrot cake, as the girls sat in the kitchen at Grace and Katie's house.

"I've been working on a book of my own," Grace revealed. "It's my project book for my Dancer badge. Would you like to see it?"

"Yes, please!" the others said.

Grace had been working towards the badge for the past month and the project book was the last bit left.

"Here." Grace fetched the scrapbook and placed it carefully on the table. "I've been finding out about the stories of lots of famous ballets, and drawing pictures of well-known ballet dancers. I've even been looking at the history of different types of dancing."

"This is fantastic," said Ellie, as she turned the pages, and the others nodded in agreement. "I love your drawings!"

"Thanks," said Grace, blushing.

Since they had been at Brownies, the five girls had enjoyed working on badges with their unit. But over the past few months, they'd also started working on their own badges. Katie was working for the Sports badge, and Ellie had almost finished her Artist badge. Charlie was aiming to complete the Friend to animals badge and Jamila had begun the Musician badge.

"Talking of badges," said Jamila, "shall we take a look at the Adventure 100 website?"

"Good idea!" said Katie. "Mum said it was OK for us to use the internet. Let's go!"

"But I haven't finished my cake yet," cried Jamila.

"Nor me," said Grace.

"Well, eat up then!" Katie giggled.

The girls gathered round the computer in Katie and Grace's living room a short while later to look at the Adventure 100 site. There was so much to see! Katie really liked the sound of "Look up High", because it included things like climbing. She was also keen on "Wet & Wild" – which involved getting around on water – because she was such a good swimmer. Everyone liked the idea of the "Future" section, as it was all about what you wanted to do when you were older. Grace and Jamila both thought that "What a Performance" sounded good because it involved singing, dancing and acting.

Then there was "Flashback", a section about how Girlguiding UK started and what it had been like over the past one hundred years, and "Moving", which was all about travel, plus "Ice Cool", which was about chilling out.

"I want to do all the tasks," Katie sighed once they'd searched the entire site.

"Me too," agreed Ellie.

"Look at this one!" said Charlie. "It's called 'Wacky 100' and it's all about crazy ideas around the number one hundred."

The girls scanned through the ideas.

"What about '100 People'? It says we could collect one hundred signatures in our *Greatest Adventure* booklet, to earn ten points. That sounds fun!" said Grace.

"I've got an even better idea!" said Charlie. "How about we collect signatures from one hundred people who've all been Brownies themselves?"

"That's genius," agreed Ellie. "But it's a lot of people to find."

“I think we should go for it.” Grace grinned. “Why don’t you tell Vicky and Sam about your idea next week?”

On Saturday afternoon, the girls met up at a birthday party with a special theme. It was for Megha, whose grandma lived next door to Katie and Grace. She didn’t go to their school, but the girls had got to know her because Megha spent a lot of time at her grandma’s.

“I’ve never been to a dance party before,” said Charlie. “What do you think happens?”

“I don’t know,” replied Grace. “But I can’t wait to find out – come on!”

The five best friends rushed into Powelbridge Community Hall, where the party was being held. There were glittery decorations, and music was already playing.

“Happy Birthday!” all the girls yelled when they saw Megha, and they handed her the presents that they’d brought.

“Thanks!” Megha grinned. “Come on – we’re about to start the dancing!”

It turned out that there was a special dance teacher, Caz, who had come to teach them the routine to a recent chart hit. Everyone had a terrific time learning all the moves, and at the end of the party, Grace and the others rushed up to Caz to thank her.

"I'm glad you enjoyed it," Caz replied. "Hey – isn't that a Brownie badge?"

She pointed to the special Centenary badge that Charlie had pinned to her T-shirt.

"How did you know that?" Katie asked.

"Well, I've been reading all about the Girlguiding UK Centenary in the papers," Caz said. "I used to be a Brownie, you know."

"Cool!" exclaimed Ellie.

"Ooh, you used to be a Brownie? Can I have your autograph?" asked Charlie.

She explained about the autograph challenge for Adventure 100, but then wailed, "Oh no! I haven't got my *Greatest Adventure* booklet with me!"

"Why don't I just sign a piece of paper," Caz suggested, taking a notebook and a pen out of her bag. "Then you can stick it into your special booklet later."

"Wow, thanks!" Charlie smiled.

"I want one too!" cried the others.

"Well, aren't I popular?" Caz giggled. "Go on then – I'll do you all a Brownie good turn!"

Chapter 3

The friends couldn't wait to talk about the website with all the other Brownies the following week. They knew that everyone else would have lots of ideas too.

"Hello, Brownies!" said Vicky and Sam, as they looked around the Ring.

"Hello!" All the girls grinned.

"So," said Sam, "has anyone got any news they'd like to tell us this week?"

Caitlin told everyone about how she was going to her big sister's school play and Ashvini said that her brother had broken his finger playing football in the garden. Then Jamila stuck up her hand.

"Jamila?" asked Vicky.

"I've just remembered that we – me, Grace, Katie, Ellie and Charlie, that is – are going to Baden-gig in the park next weekend!"

"What's Baden-gig?" asked Lottie.

"Well," said Jamila, "it's like an open-air concert where lots of new bands play. My brothers' band is performing."

"Wow," said Faith. "Are they famous?"

"My brothers?" exclaimed Jamila. "You must be joking! But I suppose they don't sound too awful. I mean, they've been practising..."

All the Brownies laughed.

Sam giggled. "Thanks, Jamila. Have a great time at the concert. So, is that all for news?"

Everyone nodded.

"OK then. Time to talk about Adventure 100! Have you had a chance to look in your *Greatest Adventure* booklets or on the website?" Vicky asked.

Every single Brownie answered at once! They were all buzzing with ideas of what they would like to do towards their Adventure 100 badge, but there was so much noise that Vicky and Sam had to put up their right hands. Gradually, every Brownie did the same and the room fell quiet.

"My goodness!" Vicky exclaimed. "I can tell that this challenge has got all of you excited! Sam and I thought we'd try to focus on just three of the sections tonight."

"Yes," agreed Sam. "We'll be concentrating on 'Future', 'Wacky 100' and 'Look up High', but let's start with 'Future'."

"The website says that 'Future' is all about what we want to be when we're older, doesn't it?" asked Megan.

"Yes, but it's also about Brownies in the future," said Faith. "Like what we think Brownies will be doing in another hundred years' time."

"That's right," said Vicky.

Pip, encouraged by Katie, put up her hand.

Vicky smiled at the newest member of the 1st Badenbridge Brownies. "Yes, Pip."

"I was thinking... One of the tasks in the 'Future' section is to do with telling people about Brownies and what we do. I thought it might be good to let some more girls know about what fun we have – if Jessica hadn't told me about the brilliant time she had at First Badenbridge Brownies, I might never have joined! Maybe we could do something to advertise Brownies."

The other girls nodded approvingly.

"Ooh!" Grace shot up her hand.

"Yes, Grace?"

"Another one of the tasks in 'Future' is to make up a dance. At the weekend, I – well, actually, it was me, Jamila, Katie, Charlie and Ellie – we went to this really brilliant party," Grace explained. "There was a dance teacher there who taught us a really cool dance routine – do you think we could make up a routine to let everyone know about Brownies for Adventure 100? It would earn us five points!"

"That's a really cool idea," agreed Caitlin, who went to dance classes with Grace.

"And if we did a good job and showed how much fun Brownies is, then loads of other girls will want to join!" said Poppy.

"Excellent," declared Sam. "Who agrees we should use Pip and Katie's ideas?"

Every Brownie in the hall put up her hand.

"Great!" said Vicky. "Now, as Grace and Caitlin are our unit dancers, how about you do the choreography?"

Grace and Caitlin grinned at each other and nodded. They'd love to do it!

"But we'll need some music," Caitlin said.

"Oh, I can think of loads of songs that I've got on CD," said Jamila, and she listed some of her favourites.

After another show of hands, the Brownies had chosen the one they liked best.

"We could write a kind of chant to go with it," suggested Poppy, who went to the same music group as Jamila.

"Good idea," said Sam. "Would you and Jamila like to have a go at writing that?"

"Yes, please!" they replied.

"Hey, we should have pompoms to shake!" Daisy added. "We had them at a swimming gala I went to a few weeks ago. We made them out of plastic bags."

"Yeaaah!" cheered the excited Brownies.

"Do you think you could teach us how to make them?" Vicky asked her daughter.

"Sure," said Daisy. "You'll all need to collect as many old plastic carrier bags as you can find and bring them to Brownies next week."

The Brownies said that they would.

"OK then," said Vicky, scribbling down everything they had talked about on her clipboard. "Sam and I will work out when we can put on our performance – probably one night after Brownies. We'll let you know at our next meeting."

Emma, Sixer of the Foxes, put up her hand.

"I'm going to see my auntie in a play at the weekend," she said. "She's in the Badenbridge Players. I read on the website that I can see a live show as part of 'What a Performance'. Will my auntie's play count?"

"Of course," said Sam. "And Baden-gig will too. If anyone else is seeing a show soon, remember that it will count towards your

Adventure 100 points if you report back to us on it!"

The Brownies nodded.

"So, what's next then?" asked Vicky.

Charlie put up her hand. "I had an idea for 'Wacky 100'!" she said. "It's for '100 Signatures'."

Charlie told them all about getting the dance teacher's autograph. "She used to be a Brownie too," she went on. "So I asked for her signature. I thought we could collect one hundred autographs of people who used to be Brownies."

"That's an ace idea!" exclaimed Lauren. "We could stick all the signatures on a big board!"

"Like an autograph wall!" added Katie. "We could have it on display for people to sign when they come to our dance performance."

The Brownies nodded in agreement.

"I could make the autograph wall," Daisy offered.

"Excellent!" declared Vicky. "So … what about 'Look up High'. Does anyone have any bright ideas for this section?"

"My grandpa works at the town hall," said Chloe. "He sometimes takes people up the clock tower there. We could do that!"

"And then hang a First Badenbridge Brownies banner from the top so that everyone can see it!" suggested Molly.

"Brilliant!" said the Brownies.

"We've still got the banner we made for our craft sale," said Sam. "Perhaps we could adapt that."

"We need to get permission to hang it from the clock tower first," warned Vicky. "I'd better have a word with Chloe's grandpa and see what he thinks – but it's a terrific idea."

Amy put up her hand. "I don't think I'd want to go up the tower," she said. "It's a bit scarily high."

"No one has to do anything they don't fancy," said Vicky. "Would some of you like to fly a kite for 'Look up High' instead?"

A few girls around the Ring nodded.

"We could put Brownie symbols on the kites!" suggested Ellie.

"I've been kite flying with the Guides," said Daisy, turning to her mum. "Would you like me to help with that?"

"Yes, please," said Vicky, writing that down on her clipboard. "Phew! We've got so many ideas, haven't we? Now, who wants to finish their dreamcatcher?" she asked.

"Meee!" said every Brownie.

"Come on then, off to your Six tables! Then we can read you the email we've had from the Second Olave Valley Guides telling us their news!"

The 2nd Olave Valley Guides were in Australia. Katie and Grace's cousin Sienna was a member, and when she had come to Badenbridge for a holiday, the Brownies had linked up with them.

"Can we write an email back, telling them about Adventure 100?" asked Sukia.

Sam looked at her watch. "OK, but we'd better be quick. Let's finish those dreamcatchers first."

Chapter 4

Grace and Caitlin couldn't wait to start creating the Brownie dance routine. The next day, as soon as the bell went for breaktime, they wasted no time in finding a spot in the playground.

"How about something like this?" suggested Grace, making a sequence of moves with her feet.

"Da da de da DAH!" sang Caitlin, joining in with Grace's steps.

"Hey, that's looking good!" said Katie, coming over with Charlie to watch Caitlin and Grace dance. The two Brownie choreographers did another twirl.

"Don't make it too complicated!" warned Charlie. "We're not all such good dancers as you two."

"We won't," said Caitlin. "Promise!"

"Oh no!" Grace wailed as the bell rang for the end of breaktime. "We were just getting into it!"

"Never mind," said Katie. "There's always lunchtime."

What with the dance routine to choreograph, the Brownie chant to write and badges to work on, the rest of the week sped by. Grace and Caitlin spent every spare second working on the steps for their routine. And on Friday, Jamila and Poppy got together after school to work on the chant.

So when the five best friends met up at Ellie's on Saturday afternoon, there was so much to talk about, they didn't know where to start!

"Hey, Grace," Jamila said. "How are you and Caitlin getting on with the dance?"

"Yeah," said Ellie. "You've spent ages working on it. Is it finished?"

"Well..." Grace said thoughtfully. "We think so! But until everyone has a go at it, we won't know if it's going to work. Hey, Jamila, how are you and Poppy getting on with the Brownie chant?"

"It's ready!" Jamila grinned. "I can't wait to see how everything works together – especially with the pompoms that Daisy's going to help us make. Have you lot got some carrier bags to take to Brownies? I've raided my mum's kitchen cupboard – she had loads in there."

Ellie giggled. "My mum had loads too. I've got bags in all the colours of the rainbow."

"Oh, I just can't wait to start learning the dance routine," said Katie. "It's going to be so much fun!"

"And it's a chance to tell everyone else how much fun Brownies is!" Ellie pointed out.

"Pip was right," said Charlie. "Her idea about telling other girls what a brilliant time we have at Brownies is great. I really hope that loads of girls will want to be Brownies once they see what a good time we have!"

"Hey, I think I've just had a fantastic idea!" Katie exclaimed. "We should have a Brownies open evening! You know – like the one we went to before we started school?"

"Of course!" exclaimed Grace. "We could do the same thing. We could invite lots of girls to come along and see all the things we do at Brownies."

"And wouldn't an open evening count as the 'Future' part of Adventure 100 too?" said Charlie.

"It might," said Grace. "There's so much that has to be done for the Adventure 100 badge, but it feels like we've already done a lot."

"And remember we're going to Baden-gig tomorrow," pointed out Jamila. "It's going to be brilliant!"

"Yaaay!" the others cheered in agreement.

Chapter 5

Jamila, Ellie, Charlie, Grace and Katie met up in the playground first thing on Monday.

"Wasn't Baden-gig the best fun ever?" said Jamila.

"Yes," agreed Ellie. "All those different bands – and the music was amazing! I can't stop singing that last song we heard."

"Plus the fireworks and the dancing," added Grace.

"I loved every minute of it," sighed Katie.

"I wish we could go all over again!" Charlie grinned.

"I wish we could be in it," said Jamila. "I'd love to perform in a big concert like that."

"I know," agreed Grace. "I mean – I'd love to dance on a stage like that huge bandstand. Imagine all those people watching and cheering you on! I wish the Brownies could do something there one day!"

"That would be so much fun!" Ellie agreed. "Maybe we could have a Brownie night there sometime."

Grace shrieked with excitement, making the other girls jump. "Hey! Maybe we should do our Brownie dance performance there! You know – our Adventure 100 dance. On the bandstand!"

"That would be perfect," agreed Jamila. "Oh yes – we've got to!"

"Do you think Vicky and Sam would be OK with it?" wondered Charlie.

"Let's ask them tomorrow at Brownies and find out," announced Grace.

On Tuesday night, all the Brownies were sitting in the Ring for their Pow Wow, catching up on each other's news. Emma was telling them about the play she'd seen her auntie in.

"I didn't realize the play had singing in it and everything!" Emma said excitedly. "My auntie played a witch and she was well wicked. Which was good really because it was called *Wicked*!"

"It sounds brilliant," replied Vicky. "Well

done Emma for reporting back so enthusiastically. I almost feel like I was there with you! Now … I think that Jamila, Charlie, Ellie, Katie and Grace went to Baden-gig, didn't you? Why don't you tell us about that?"

Jamila told everyone about her brothers' band.

"They were quite good actually," she said. "Even if they are my brothers!"

The Brownies giggled.

"Yes," added Ellie. "There were lots of other bands too – they were all good."

"One of them was a girl band," Katie explained.

"And at the end of the concert there was a fireworks display with music to go with it," said Charlie.

"And there were all these dancers on the bandstand too!" said Grace. "They were

amazing. And it made me think – it made *us* think – wouldn't it be really cool for us to do our Adventure 100 Brownie dance routine on the bandstand in the park!"

There was a gasp of excitement from around the hall.

"Yes!" Jasmine exclaimed. "We could do it in front of loads of people then!"

"Wow," Caitlin sighed. "I'd love to dance on the bandstand."

"It would be so cool," agreed Sukia.

"Do you think we could?" wondered Pip.

"It would certainly be a special place to perform," said Sam thoughtfully.

"Hey – in 'Wacky 100' there's a bit called '100 Pennies' where you collect pennies for charity. If we did our routine on the bandstand and lots of people saw us, maybe we could ask for a penny from each person in the audience," Ashvini pointed out.

"Yesss!" cheered the Brownies around the Ring.

"And we could have our autograph wall up too," added Charlie. "That's for 'Wacky 100' as well!"

Grace grinned. She'd had no idea that everyone would think her idea was *that* good – nor that everyone's ideas for other tasks would tie in with it so well!

"Oooh!" Jamila shot up her hand. "Vicky! Sam! Why don't we do our dance routine in other places too?"

"How do you mean?" Sam wondered.

"Well," said Jamila, "maybe we could dance in the town square and maybe the library – we could dash all around town and dance!"

"We could call it Dance Dash!" said Daisy.

Now the Brownies were clapping with excitement. It was a completely brilliant idea!

"Vicky!" Katie shot up her hand. "We had another thought, too. We were talking about how girls find out about Brownies," Katie explained. "And we were thinking that we could have a special night when we asked girls who aren't Brownies yet if they wanted to come along and see what we get up to at our meetings."

“Like an open evening?” asked Sam. “That’s another good suggestion!”

There was a murmur of agreement from the others.

“And we could hand out leaflets about it at our Dance Dash!” pointed out Izzy.

“Perfect,” declared Vicky, scribbling down all the girls’ ideas on her clipboard. “What an imaginative bunch of Brownies you are!”

"Yes," said Sam. "Now we'd better get ourselves organized so that we can make it all work. Vicky, Daisy and I will put our thinking caps on and get back to you about everything next week. Meantime…"

The Brownies looked up at her excitedly.

"We've got some news about the clock tower. We've been told we can climb it, so we'll have some letters for you to take home about it this evening. We've also got a letter about the kite flying for the girls who would like to do that. Ask at home if you can come and then get someone to sign the permission slip and return it next week."

Jamila, Katie, Ellie, Grace and Charlie looked at each other and grinned. They couldn't wait to climb the clocktower!

"Now, tonight," announced Vicky, "Grace and Caitlin are going to start teaching us the dance routine. *And* Daisy is helping us make our pompoms. Which means we've got lots to get through before home time!"

"Who's remembered their carrier bags?" asked Daisy.

"Me!" yelled every Brownie in the Ring.

"Come on then." Daisy giggled. "Let's get busy!"

"Quick!" said Katie to Pip. "Let's do ours together."

Chapter 6

The girls loved Grace and Caitlin's dance routine. Every break time, all the Brownies that went to their school gathered in the playground to practise. Katie gave Pip as much help as she needed to learn the steps. The girls who weren't Brownies came over to see what they were up to because the dance routine looked like such good fun. So the Brownies told them about the open evening that was happening soon and said they should come along and find out what other brilliant things they got up to at their meetings.

The girls still needed to make a second pompom each, so on Saturday, Ellie, Charlie,

Grace and Katie met up at Jamila's house for a craft session.

"I've raided my mum's stash of plastic carrier bags again," said Jamila.

"Great," said Charlie. "Let's start cutting them into strips."

Jamila's mum sat with them whilst they snipped away to make piles of brightly coloured plastic strips. Then they tied the strips together at one end to make a handle.

"Now that you've finished cutting," she said after a while, "who fancies a milkshake?"

"Me!" the five friends chanted.

Jamila's mum giggled. "I'll be back in a minute then."

"These will look great," Charlie announced, as the girls finished their pompoms, and their milkshakes, a short while later.

"I can't wait to practise with them at Brownies on Tuesday!" Ellie grinned, shaking her pompom above her head.

"Nor me," agreed Grace. "We're doing so many things for the Adventure 100 badge already – and we've got a whole year to finish it."

"Hey, do you think we could do all the tasks in all the sections?" asked her sister.

"But there are *tons* of tasks for this badge!" said Jamila in amazement.

"Do you think your mum will let us take a look on the Adventure 100 website now?" Katie asked. She was beginning to wonder if she could be the first Brownie in the country to finish her Adventure 100 badge!

"I'll go and ask her," said Jamila, racing off.

A few minutes later, the five friends were surfing the Adventure 100 website, checking out the section called "Ice Cool".

"I'm not sure I like the idea of a winter camp-out," said Ellie, shivering at the thought.

"But I *do* like the idea of having a food party with lots of chilly cold food," Jamila replied, licking her lips.

"How about the 'Cool Threads' swap-it party?" suggested Grace. "It says you can bring clothes to a party and swap them for some different ones."

"But I like all my clothes!" said Charlie. "I don't *want* to swap them!"

"No one would make you do that." Jamila giggled.

Katie grinned. "Hey, Ellie," she said, "if you don't like the idea of sleeping out in winter, how about breaking the record of how many jumpers you could wear at once?"

They all burst out laughing at the thought of how silly they'd look.

"How about this one?" said Ellie, pointing at the screen. "'Cool Chat'."

The girls stopped talking to read about the tasks in that section.

"How can we learn texting?" asked Grace.

"We don't have mobile phones!"

"And I don't think I could work out a secret code, let alone make one up," sighed Charlie.

"But we can *speak* on the phone, can't we," said Ellie.

"Course we can," said Jamila. "Except it says that we've got to speak to someone abroad over the internet. Who do we know abro—"

And before Jamila could finish, all the others yelled "*Sienna!*"

"I know!" said Ellie. "Mum put Skype on to her computer a few weeks ago – she uses it to phone her cousin in Canada."

"Do you think she'd let us phone Sienna?" wondered Charlie. "It would be so cool."

Ellie nodded. "I'm sure she would!"

"Er – small problem," said Katie, holding

her hands up. "Australia has night-time when we have daytime!"

"Oh no," said Ellie. "I hadn't thought of that."

It looked like the girls' next big idea had gone wrong before they'd even made a start.

"Hang on," Grace said. "Sometimes our mum has spoken to my auntie really late at night. I mean, it's really late here and really early in the morning in Australia – so everyone is awake!"

"Excellent!" Ellie replied. "All we've got to do is email Sienna and arrange a time to chat, then have a sleepover and ring her before we go to bed! That would give us another ten points towards our Adventure 100 goal!"

"Yesss!" cheered the five best friends.

They couldn't wait!

Chapter 7

Jamila, Ellie, Charlie, Katie and Grace took their pompoms to Brownies on Tuesday night.

"Don't they look terrific!" said Daisy, as all the girls gathered in the hall, shaking their pompoms above their heads.

"Hey, Pip!" said Katie. "Yours are so colourful – they look great!"

"Thanks!" Pip grinned, giving them a shake.

As soon as all the Brownies had arrived, Vicky suggested that they started the evening with a rehearsal of the dance routine. But first, everyone had to learn the words that Jamila and Poppy had written to go with it. So, the Brownies formed a Ring and sat down to learn the chant. After a few tries, they had it memorized!

Brownies are cool
Brownies are great
It's the Brownie and Guide Centenary
Come and Celebrate!

B – R – O – W – N – I – E – S

BROWNIES!

The Brownies sang out with enthusiasm.

"Fantastic!" said Sam. "Well done, Poppy and Jamila. That rhyme is sure to get everyone's attention!"

"Shall we try the dance with the words now?" urged Caitlin.

"And the pompoms," said Ellie, shaking hers excitedly.

"OK," said Grace. "Let's get in our lines: tallest Brownies at the back, smallest in the front. Ready? One, two, three and..."

The Brownies, who had become perfect at the routine, started off with great energy. But now that the girls had the words *and* the pompoms, as well as the dance steps to remember, some of them were getting confused. Some were brilliant at the words but couldn't do the steps as well. Others got the steps but dropped their pompoms.

"Oh no!" wailed Grace when everyone ground to a halt before the routine was even finished. "Shall we start again?"

But the same thing happened – and this time, some of the Brownies began to giggle.

"This is a bit of a pickle," said Caitlin.

"This is a disaster! We're never going to get this right, and we'll look silly in front of all those people!" Grace said, her eyes filling with tears.

"Hey, Grace," said Jamila, putting a comforting hand on her friend's shoulder. "It'll be fine. It's just that we're not as brilliant at dancing as you and Caitlin."

"Yes," agreed Ellie. "We just need a bit longer to learn it."

"Then it will be terrific!" said Sukia.

Grace smiled weakly.

"Tell you what," suggested Vicky. "Why don't we have our Pow Wow now? Then we can go back to rehearsing the dance routine afterwards."

So the Brownies quickly sat down in the Ring.

"Now, girls," said Vicky, looking at her clipboard. "We've only got time for a quick Pow Wow this evening."

"There's good news about our Dance Dash," said Sam. "We can tell you all the locations we've got permission for..."

Grace crossed her fingers. Even though she was still worried that the routine would go wrong and be a total embarrassment, she really wanted to dance at the bandstand.

"We've spoken to the council, and they've agreed to us dancing at the library, outside the supermarket, at the bandstand—"

"Yes!" Grace cheered, making the others laugh.

"And the town hall," finished Sam.

"But we have to stay in the area that's just in front of the town hall steps or we might get in people's way," warned Vicky.

"We've also got news about our Brownie banner," said Sam.

She stood up and, with Vicky holding the other end, they showed the Brownies the banner they'd adapted.

The girls agreed that the sign looked brilliant.

"Glad you like it." Vicky smiled. "So, who's brought their permission slips for the clock-tower climb and the kite flying this Saturday?"

Most of the Brownies put up their hands.

"Great!" said Vicky. "We'll all meet up at the town hall in the morning. Sam and Daisy will take some of you to fly kites, and the rest of us will be with Sukia's mum and Chloe's grandad, climbing to the top of the tower!"

The Brownies chattered excitedly.

"So," said Sam, looking at her watch. "We've still got some more dance practice to do and then we'll decorate the kites I've brought with me. Let's get busy!"

The Brownies decided Grace and Caitlin should go through the routine in front of everyone, just to remind all the girls what they were meant to do.

Then the Brownies got into their dance

lines again and, with Daisy starting the music, the girls got dancing, singing and waving their pompoms.

Even though a couple of girls dropped pompoms and turned the wrong way, it went pretty well. After a couple more run-throughs, the routine was almost perfect.

Sam clapped. "That was so much better."

The Brownies gave themselves a cheer, and Grace and Caitlin smiled at each other, relieved.

"Right," said Vicky. "We thought it might be fun if everyone helped to decorate the kites, even the girls who are climbing the tower instead. We've put them out ready on your Six tables, and we've got these Brownie stickers to decorate them with. Let's all get stuck in, shall we?"

The Brownies rushed over to help.

It was almost time to go home.

"Already?" sighed Jasmine. "But we're having so much fun!"

"Into the Ring, please – quickly, girls!" urged Vicky. "We've got to decide what you'd like to wear for Dance Dash."

"Won't we wear our Brownie clothes?" asked Holly.

"Well," said Sam. "Brownie T-shirts, yes. But what would you like to wear with them?"

"I've got some red jazz pants from dance class," said Caitlin. "But not everyone will have those."

"How about bright leggings and stripy legwarmers?" suggested Grace.

"Yes!" agreed all the others.

"And maybe we could wear sparkly bracelets and headbands too," Ellie said.

"So Brownie tops and your own bright leggings and sparkly things then?" Vicky grinned. "Excellent – can you start organizing your outfits?"

The Brownies nodded eagerly.

"Great! And if you bring your clothes along next Tuesday, we can have a dress rehearsal," said Vicky.

"Now, before the end of tonight's meeting, we've got some things to hand out," announced Sam. "First are the Dance Dash posters..."

She passed them around the Ring so that each Brownie had a copy.

"We've designed it in black and white so that you can each colour in and decorate your own one," Sam explained. "Once you've finished it, we'd like you to find somewhere in town to put it up where lots of people will see it. Remember, the more people who see the posters, the more people will come to Dance Dash!"

"And I've got this letter about Dance Dash for you," said Vicky. "It's got all the details about where you all have to be and when. Make sure you get the permission slip signed and bring it back next week."

"Now," said Sam. "I can see people are waiting to take you all home. Come on, let's sing Brownie Bells."

In the Ring, all the Brownies linked hands before they sang the final song of the meeting.

Chapter 8

The girls gathered at Ellie's house after school on Wednesday to colour in their posters.

"You've got tons of really brilliant coloured pens," said Charlie enviously.

"Thanks." Ellie smiled. She loved everything arty. "Do you think I'll be able to use my poster as part of my Artist badge?"

"Maybe," said Katie. "Hey, what do you think of the colour of my lettering?"

"Cool!" exclaimed the others.

The girls worked carefully – they wanted their posters to look especially eye-catching so that everyone in Badenbridge would know about Dance Dash.

"I can't wait until we get to dance in front of all those people!" sighed Grace, as she put some glitter star stickers on her poster to finish it off.

"I can't wait to climb the clock tower," Katie replied. "It's going to be so high – and so cool!"

"Come on," Ellie said. "Let's finish these off and then have tea!"

On Thursday after school, Jamila, Charlie, Katie, Grace and Ellie set off on an expedition to put up the posters all around Badenbridge. Jamila's mum was with them as they headed off down the high street.

"Other Brownies have been here already!" said Katie, as she pointed to at least three shops with posters in their front windows.

"Oh yes," sighed Ellie.

"How about the doctor's surgery?" suggested Grace.

"And the nursery school and the dentist?" added Charlie.

"Plus there's the supermarket noticeboard," Jamila pointed out.

"Don't forget the board at the park entrance – and the garden centre too!" finished Ellie.

"There're loads of places for us to try," said Katie. "Come on – let's get going!"

It was raining when they woke up on Saturday morning but, fortunately, the sky had cleared and the sun was shining by the time they all met up with Vicky, Sam, Daisy and Sukia's mum outside the town hall.

"Right," said Vicky, after she'd checked everyone's names off the list. "Kite flyers with Daisy and Sam, please. Everyone else with us."

Jamila, Grace, Ellie, Charlie and Katie all followed Vicky as they entered a special door at the side of the clock tower.

"I didn't even know this door was here," Katie said to Charlie.

"Hello, Brownies!" said a smiley man with white hair.

"This is Mr Bunting – Chloe's grandpa!" explained Vicky. "He's come to show us the way."

"Morning, Mr Bunting!" cheered the excited girls.

"Morning, Grandpa!" Chloe giggled.

"Good morning!" he replied. "Now, you've got one hundred and thirty steps to climb. I do it once a week to check on the clock, so it's nice to have some company for a change. Take it slowly, hold on to the hand rail – and follow me!"

"I want to be the first to the top!" Katie declared, pushing her way to the front. "Come on!" she urged her four best friends.

"And me!" announced Pip excitedly.

"Come on then!" Katie grinned at her. "You go in front – we can be the first Brownies to the top!"

"One, two, three, four…" Pip counted out loud as she climbed the spiral of stairs. "Hey – it's a really long way up there!"

The Brownies looked up and saw a light that seemed hundreds of metres away.

"Hello!" Izzy called up into the roof.

The Brownies giggled as they heard her voice echo above them.

After a while, Pip slowed down, panting. Mr Bunting steamed ahead.

"What's up?" asked Katie.

"I can't do it," said Pip, looking down. "Oh no – it's such a long way back down. And ages before we reach the top. And it's so small in here – I can't!"

"It's OK," soothed Katie. "Come on – let's keep going or we'll lose Chloe's grandpa."

"What's the matter?" asked Vicky, who was a few Brownies behind them.

The other girls started to chatter, wondering what the hold-up was.

"I've got to go back down!" Pip panicked. "I can't do it!"

"Hey," said Grace soothingly. "You'll be OK – promise."

"Do you want me to come back down with you?" suggested Vicky.

Pip stood, pale-faced on the steps. "I don't know."

Pip wasn't sure why, but she felt scared. Scared that she couldn't reach the top of the tower and scared about falling. But she didn't want to let the Brownies, especially Katie, down.

"Shall I come back with you?" asked Katie.

She didn't really want to give up and lose out on the points that she'd earn for her Adventure 100 badge. But she wanted to do her Brownie best – and that meant making sure Pip was OK.

Pip looked at Katie, wide-eyed.

"No – yes – I don't know..." Pip breathed.

"Everything OK, Brownies?" Mr Bunting called down the spiral staircase. "You're doing really well – we're nearly there!"

"Come on," said Katie. "How about I go in front and hold your hand. We can do it together."

Pip looked at her, uncertain.

"And I'll be right behind you," said Jamila.

"Ready?" asked Katie.

Pip looked at her Brownie Buddy.

"You can do it, Pip!" cheered Ellie.

"OK," Pip gulped. "Let's do it!"

And with the support of all her Brownie friends, Pip climbed to the top.

"Wow! This is amazing!" said Pip, as the girls looked down at all of Badenbridge from the top of the clock tower. "Thanks so much for helping me get up here and see it, Katie."

"No worries." Katie smiled. "I'm just really pleased we all made it up. It's fantastic, isn't it?"

As the Brownies took in the sights of the town, Mr Bunting and Vicky tied the Brownie banner to the balcony railings.

"Hey!" exclaimed Amber. "I can see the others flying their kites in the park – look!"

The other Brownies gathered to see where she was pointing.

"You can even see the Brownie symbols on some of them!" added Lauren.

"And look," pointed out Holly. "They've just spotted our banner too – they're waving!"

"This is brilliant, isn't it?" Vicky grinned.

"Yes!" the Brownies agreed.

After climbing back down safely, and meeting up with the kite-flying Brownies, the five best friends made their way back to Ellie's house with her mum. They were going to have their sleepover and speak to Sienna!

"Was Pip all right?" Charlie asked, concerned.

"Fine now, thanks," said a grateful Katie. "She just got a bit worried up there."

"But you were great with her." Jamila hugged her friend.

"Brownies always do their best, don't they?" Ellie grinned.

"Because Brownies *are* the best!" exclaimed Grace.

"Hey," said Charlie thoughtfully. "Do you

know – with the Centenary party, the dreamcatchers, Baden-gig, the posters and the clock-tower climb, we've already got thirty-five points towards our Adventure 100 badge!"

"Then there's Dance Dash – and we're calling Sienna in Australia tonight as well," Ellie pointed out.

"How cool is that!" said Jamila.

"It's 'Ice Cool' – like the challenge!" giggled Charlie, and her friends laughed along with her.

It was after midnight when the five friends saw Sienna smiling at them from Ellie's mum's computer screen.

"We had a great day today," explained Katie, telling her cousin all about their Brownie adventure so far.

"Excellent!" Sienna smiled. "We've been doing lots of stuff for the Centenary too."

"What sort of things?" Charlie wanted to know.

"We've had an international camp with Guides from all over Australia and other countries," revealed Sienna. "There were lots of activities and music, and I made so many new friends. Plus I've got a special Centenary badge. Have you got one too?"

"Course – look!" Ellie picked up her own Centenary badge from the table and held it up to the webcam. "Perhaps we can swap one for yours?"

"Good idea," said Sienna.

After chatting for a few minutes longer, Jamila let out an enormous yawn.

"I guess we'd better go." Grace giggled. "Before we all fall asleep!"

"OK. But make sure you call me again soon!" urged Sienna. "Bye!"

"Bye!" the five sleepy friends said in reply, waving at the computer screen.

Chapter 9

On Tuesday night at Brownies, the five best friends told everyone about their phone call, and the idea of the badge swap.

"Looks like you've earned some more points for your 'Cool Chat'," said Sam, noting it down in her book. "You've done well!"

"Yes, everyone's been working really hard," added Vicky. "We had lots of compliments from people after our 'Look up High' challenges on Saturday!"

Sam grinned. "Now, has everyone brought their outfits for Dance Dash along with them today?"

"Yes!" the Brownies replied excitedly.

"Excellent! Well, let's see them! Then we can get on with our dress rehearsal for Dance Dash this weekend."

The final rehearsal was brilliant! Everyone remembered their steps and the words, and shook their pompoms perfectly.

"That was great!" said Daisy, who had been watching them all.

"Really?" said Grace hopefully.

"Really!" Daisy replied. "And your outfits are fantastic! You're all so colourful and sparkly."

"No one will be able to miss you dancing, and I'm sure they'll all want to donate pennies," Vicky added.

"Vicky," Izzy said, "if we're collecting pennies from people as we dash around, how are we going to take the coins and dance?"

"Sam and I thought we could carry the buckets," said Vicky. "That way you girls can focus on your dancing."

"Who are we collecting the pennies for?" asked Pip.

"Well, we thought we could donate them to the Guide Friendship Fund," Sam replied.

"What's that?" asked Amber.

"It helps fund things for Brownie and Guide units in the UK and abroad," said Daisy. "We collected money for it at Guides. The fund also helps units in countries where natural disasters – like floods – have happened."

"That sounds good," said Lottie.

"Who agrees we should donate the money to the Guide Friendship Fund, then?" Vicky asked.

All the Brownies put up their hands.

"Agreed!" Vicky grinned.

"OK!" Sam said. "Let's sort out the buckets and then we can have our Pow Wow."

Daisy made the first announcement in the Pow Wow.

"We've had an email from the Second Olave Valley Guides," she said. "It says 'Hi, First Badenbridge Brownies! Good luck with Dance Dash – it's a fantastic idea! We hope it goes well. Have fun!'"

The Brownies smiled at one another.

"Now, have you all remembered to bring

your permission slips back?" asked Sam.

The girls all nodded and held them out for her to collect.

"Daisy is going to help us on Saturday by handing out leaflets about the open evening you suggested, Katie," Vicky explained.

Katie grinned.

"We'll be holding it next week, so our next Brownie meeting will be all about showing girls what we get up to," said Sam.

"Cool!" said the Brownies.

"So," asked Vicky. "Is everyone happy with all the details for Saturday?"

The Brownies nodded.

"See you at Dance Dash, then!"

Chapter 10

At last, it was Dance Dash day! The Brownies gathered at Badenbridge Primary School, waiting excitedly to set off for town. As soon as everyone had arrived, Sam took a roll call.

"Have we got the buckets? The autograph wall? Our pompoms? Our best Brownie voices and dancing feet?" asked Vicky.

"Yesss!" cheered the Brownies.

"So what are we waiting for?" Sam grinned. "Let's Dance Dash!"

Everyone was really nervous before they did the first dance, but they had no reason to be. When they arrived at the supermarket, people were bustling about with their shopping, but as soon as the Brownies got into position and the music started, they stopped to watch. Some began to sway to the beat, and a few girls even tried to join in!

As the Brownies danced, their audience put pennies into the collection buckets, and Daisy

handed out sheets about the open evening. She made sure that the girls who'd been so keen to dance and sing with them got copies.

"BROWNIES!" the girls cheered at the end, and the audience applauded enthusiastically.

So enthusiastically, in fact, that they decided to dance the routine once more! Then it was time for a break. The Brownies were grateful for the chance to get their breath back and have a drink.

"Please sign our autograph wall!" Katie urged. "Especially if you've been a Brownie!"

"And take some information about our open evening!" added Ellie. "Would you like to come to Brownies?" She handed a leaflet to a girl who was smiling at her. "We'd love to see you!"

The girls then headed to the library. The crowd there wasn't as big as the one at the supermarket, but the cheering and clapping was just as enthusiastic.

"You are so good!" declared Daisy, joining in the applause. "Come on – who's going to help me to carry the autograph wall this time?"

"I will," said Charlie. "Are we off to the town hall now?"

"Yes!" replied Vicky. "Not far to go."

The square in front of the town hall was quite busy and people began to notice the

Brownies as soon as they arrived and started to set up their dance area.

"Who's that?" Jamila asked Grace, pointing to a lady who was holding a microphone in her hand. "I saw her watching us at the library too."

"I don't know," said Grace. "Maybe she's someone's mum? Come on – it's almost time to start!"

The Brownies stood in line and waved their pompoms in the air. Daisy started the music … and the dance routine began!

"Hooray!" the crowd cheered as they finished.

Katie, Grace, Jamila, Ellie and Charlie hugged each other excitedly. Dance Dash was such good fun!

"Hello, girls!" said a voice behind them. "I see you remembered some of my steps!"

"Caz!" Grace said delightedly. She instantly recognized the lady who had taught them the dance routine at Megha's party. "Did you see our dance just then?"

"I certainly did." Caz grinned. "You were brilliant! And I love the pompoms!" She fished in her purse. "Would you like these pennies for your collection?"

"Thanks," said Ellie.

"Well, I must go now," Caz said. "Great to see you again – and keep dancing. Good luck with your Brownie challenge!"

"Bye!" The girls waved as she walked away.

"Wasn't it great to see her?" said Grace.

The others nodded.

"It's going really well, isn't it?" said Jamila.

"We're collecting lots of money in the buckets." Katie grinned.

"And the autograph wall is almost full," Charlie pointed out.

"Hey, that lady with the microphone is talking to Vicky and Sam," said Jamila.

"I wonder *who* she is...?" puzzled Katie.

The Brownies were amazed that the morning had gone so quickly, and that they were already at their last venue. Being up on the bandstand suddenly made them all realize how big it was and they felt a bit nervous. There was a big crowd waiting for their final

performance, including lots of friends and family.

"Go, Brownies!" called out Vicky and Sam as the music began and the girls started to sway to the beat.

Tapping their feet, the Brownies launched into the most energetic dance of the day. They jumped higher and shook their pompoms harder than ever.

Brownies are cool
Brownies are great
It's the Brownie and Guide Centenary
Come and Celebrate!

B – R – O – W – N – I – E – S
BROWNIES!

That was it – the last Brownie Dance Dash routine was over!

"That was so much fun!" said Grace.

"And it was all thanks to you – it was your idea!" Ellie grinned.

"No," Grace replied, "everyone had the ideas – Pip had the idea of telling people about Brownies, Jamila had the idea of the Dance Dash, Caitlin and I worked on the dance together, and then Jamila chose the music and she and Poppy wrote the chant."

"Yes," said Jamila. "Everyone did their best – just like Brownies should."

At that moment, Vicky and Sam came over to the group of excited Brownies. The lady with the microphone was with them.

"This is Suzy," Sam explained. "She's from Radio Badenbridge and she's making a special programme about the Centenary."

“Cool!” said all the Brownies.

“I’ve loved watching your Dance Dash!” said Suzy. “I’ve been talking to some of the people in the crowd as well – they’ve been telling me their memories from when they were Brownies and Guides.”

“Suzy was wondering if you’d be able to perform your Brownie chant one more time?” Vicky asked.

“Yes,” said Suzy. “I’d like to record it to play on the programme. Would that be OK?”

Would it? The Brownies were delighted to be recorded and sang at the top of their voices.

“Perfect!” Suzy exclaimed when they’d finished. “Thanks, Brownies!”

"When is the programme going to be on the radio?" Charlie asked.

"Tomorrow afternoon," Suzy said. "It's called *Suzy's Sunday Special*. I hope you like it – bye, and thanks!"

"That was an amazing morning," sighed Grace.

"I loved every minute of it," agreed Katie.

"Yes," said Jamila, "but I'm starving!"

The others laughed.

"Good job we've got a picnic to eat then," said Daisy, pointing to a huge spread of food, laid out on the picnic tables in the park, near the bandstand.

"Wow!" said Charlie.

"Come on, girls!" urged Sam. "We thought you deserved a picnic after all that activity this morning."

"Yesss!" Every single 1st Badenbridge Brownie cheered as they rushed over to the picnic tables.

On Sunday afternoon, Jamila, Charlie, Katie, Ellie and Grace gathered together at Charlie and Boo's house to listen to *Suzy's Sunday Special*. It was over an hour before Suzy mentioned the Brownies and the girls had almost given up hope of the Dance Dash report even coming on. But then suddenly they heard themselves singing.

"Shush!" hissed Katie.

The girls sat in silence, listening to Suzy talking to lots of adults who told stories about their own time in the Brownies and Guides. The piece ended with the Brownies singing their song again.

Charlie giggled. "How cool was that?"

"That was brilliant," Katie agreed.

"I can't believe how every adventure we have with Brownies is even better than the last," sighed Jamila.

"Nor me," said Grace. "Plus Vicky said that with Dance Dash, I've finished my Dancer badge. She'll award it to me next week!"

"*And* we've got *another* adventure on Tuesday, haven't we?" pointed out Ellie.

"Oh yes, the open evening. I hope loads of girls come," said Jamila. "Brownies is so brilliant. I love it!"

"Me too!" the others replied, all at the same time. Then they collapsed into happy giggles, impatient for their next Brownie meeting.

How Grace got her Dancer badge!

1. She helped choreograph the Dance Dash routine and performed it in public.

2. Grace put together a scrap book about dancing:

⋆ She stuck in lots of pictures of dancers that she'd found in magazines and newspapers.

⋆ She drew pictures of famous ballet dancers.

⋆ She wrote up a short history of different types of dancing: ballet, tap, modern and Morris dancing.

⋆ She found out the stories of some famous ballets and retold them in her book.

Dancer

How to Make a Dance Dash Pompom!

You will need:

Plastic shopping bags (brightly coloured ones are best)
A ruler
Some scissors
Some sticky tape
Some coloured string or ribbon

1. Cut the bottom and handles off the bags but keep the handles to one side as you will use these later. Take great care with scissors because they are sharp – you might want to ask an adult to help you with the cutting bit.

2. Cut the remainder of the bag into strips about 3 cm wide and 30 cm long. The number of strips you have depends on how many carrier bags you use – three to four carrier bags should make enough strips for two pompoms.

3. Divide your strips into two even piles, making sure there is an even split of coloured strips in each pile.

4. Holding the end of one of the piles, tie the strips together with the old handle of one of the bags. The best place to make the tie is at the top of your fist as you are holding the end – this will be the new handle of your pompom! Wrap the loose ends of the bag handle around the new handle of the pompom and, if necessary, secure with sticky tape.

5. To make your handle look stylish you can wrap coloured string or ribbon around it, securing it with a bit of sticky tape.

6. Scrunch the loose ends of your pompoms with your fingers so that they are crinkly and fluffy.

7. Now do the same with the other pile of strips so that you have a pair of pompoms!

Collect the other books in the series!

And look out for...

Christmas is coming, and the 1st Badenbridge Brownies are getting in to the spirit of things! With crafts to make for the local Christmas market, festive goodies to bake for the unit party, and a trip to the local pantomime to look forward to, the girls eagerly set about spreading Christmas cheer. Now, if only it would snow…